Queen Boss Slay

Patrick C. Harrison III

This is a work of fiction. None of the people, places, or events described in this novel actually exist or happened. And for the love of God, it's fiction. Calm down.

PC3 HORROR

Full Contact Fiction

pc3horror.com
Instagram@thepc3
Etsy.com/shop/pc3books
Slasher@PC3
pc3horror.substack.com
pc3@pc3horror.com

Cover design by Don Noble

Copyright © 2024 Patrick C. Harrison III

All rights reserved.

DEDICATION

For all the ladies out there.
To hell with the fellas.

CONTENTS

The Problem of Leftovers 3

Take it Easy 10

That Time of the Morning 21

Choices, Choices 33

Real Work Sucks, and So Do Men 39

The Palace of Mirrors and Grunters 48

Drama at the Pharmacy 64

Hanging With My Bestie 76

Fetch Me an Orgasm 92

Two Hunky Visitors 99

Queen Boss Slays 108

I May Have Lied 133

ACKNOWLEDGMENTS

This book would not exist without the unbelievable success of *100% Match*. So, to the thousands of readers of that nasty little book, congratulations. Because of you, something far worse has been created. And apparently, it's going to continue, because the author, the reviled PC3, has seen fit to make a series of these Pocket Nasties.

The Problem of Leftovers

Disposing of the body is probably the toughest part. We ladies can find willing helpers for a lot of things, but getting rid of a dead guy—not so easy-peasy.

Got a flat tire? No problem! Pull your shirt down a little bit, showing off your cleavage, and bend over with your ass in the air to inspect the flat, and like cattle stampeding to a trough full of feed, you'll have every swinging dick on the highway pulling over to lend a hand. Even for a girl like me, who admittedly looks pretty mid compared to your average TikTok booty-shaker, it works every time.

But a dead body problem in your recording studio can't be resolved in quite the same manner. You can't go flag down some random asshole and think they're going to assist you in a multi-felony adventure. Even if all their brains are in their ballsacks (which is the case for pretty much any guy between the ages of fifteen and forty-nine), they might question whether chopping a dead dude into pieces and stuffing said pieces into plastic bags and then burying said pieces in various locations . . . is *really* worth the trouble for the slim chance they'll get laid.

Which they won't. Not by me anyway. What you do with your vagina is up to you, though.

That's not to say I don't have sex occasionally, but we'll get to that later. Right now, I've got to dispose of this body.

Basements are rare in this part of the country, but I'm lucky enough to have one with almost equal the square footage as the house above. This is where my livestream studio is. Transporting the unconscious down the steps leading from my kitchen is tiresome, loud, and often results in waking the unknowing star of the show. So, three years ago I had a small elevator installed in the hall closet.

I paid for this with the money I received from a married father of four who enjoyed weekly sessions of having raw meat shoved up his ass while I screamed at him to finish his dinner or he couldn't go outside to play. He eventually died from a double-whammy of salmonella and dysentery.

The dominatrix garb I wore for today's performance is discarded in the laundry basket, and now, wearing only a bra and panties, I take a hazmat suit from the linen closet. I'll take a nice long shower later anyway, but the suit prevents extra gunk from reaching my pores during the disposal process; a fair amount is already splattered across my flesh from the performance.

After donning the hazmat suit, I scoop the organs off the concrete floor with a snow shovel and deposit them in a black garbage bag. The organs that remain in the body cavity, of which there are few, I remove with a pair of sheers and toss them in the bag as well. I set the bag aside and make a mental note to feed some of these remains to my dog, Howler, for dinner and to divide up the rest in Tupperware bowls for later feedings.

The hollowed-out specimen atop the surgical table is still too large to move without risking a back injury that could relegate me to the couch for the better part of a month. He was a bit hefty before his demise, not to mention dim-witted and desperate.

I could slice off some fat and use it for various products, like cooking oils, lip balms, candles, and moisturizers, but making such things is tedious and not particularly profitable. I know because I tried. The cost of tables at flea markets and conventions these days is absurd, and the customers at such functions expect dollar store prices.

So I don't bother with the fat. I could slice off a chunk or two for Howler, but he needs to lose a few pounds.

Cutting through bone can be a real chore. I'm stronger than your average chick, whose daily physical exertion moments don't exceed holding the phone in the air long enough to snap the right duck-faced bimbo pic. I exercise, though nothing major. But chopping or sawing through bone is tiresome for anybody.

There used to be this neighborhood kid who was a high school track and field star. His name was Troy, and he was always making eyes at me when he ran past as I was tending the yard or checking the mail. Guess he liked shapely ladies in their thirties, I don't know. But I figured, on account of his attraction to me, I could convince him to help me with a certain dead body problem.

You see where this is going, don't you? Yeah, you remember how this conversation started.

I convinced Troy to come inside and take off his clothes so they wouldn't get soiled. Nice body. Hard as a rock—*everything* was hard as a rock. Then I convinced him to follow me to the basement. His pencil turned into a wet noodle real quick when he saw Lyle, the dead guy, on the surgical table. I couldn't get him to saw even one limb off. Instead, he bolted up the stairs and out of the basement, his tallywhacker smacking from one muscular thigh to the other. Then he bolted out the front door, naked as the day he was vomited from his mother's twat.

Luckily, Miles, my next-door neighbor, a Vietnam vet who was always perched on his porch with a shotgun across his lap, blasted Troy down as he ran across his lawn. Miles didn't like kids on his lawn. But . . . that's not why he shot the boy, I don't think. That probably had something to do with me coming out the door screaming that Troy tried to rape me.

The cops bought it. Troy was black and the responding officers were, well, pasty white and not track and field fans. All the same, thank Christ they didn't nose around in the basement.

Anyway, a plasma cutter. I pull that out of the closet and get to work. That's the way to go when cutting up a body. Melts right through bone.

Then I double-bag the body parts and throw them in the dumpster behind the local vegan restaurant. Not even starving, homeless lepers dig through vegan garbage.

That's how you deal with your leftover body problems.

My name is Sara Martin, by the way, and my dad raped me when I was six.

Take it Easy

After a wild session, you want to give yourself time to decompress, a day or two to relax and get your energy back. I enjoy what I do, certainly, but it can be rigorous and exhausting, especially if heavy power tools are involved.

Trust me, your first time, you're going to be so excited you may not even notice the soreness and lethargy that typically sets in after a long, drawn-out session. Hell, you might be a pretty fit chick. Maybe you do yoga or run marathons or go to the gym and do squats with your fat ass facing a camera. Maybe you do all three!

That's fine and dandy, but once you start smashing bones with an eight-pound sledgehammer or repeatedly punching your gasoline-soaked, gloved hand into a guy's asshole until it looks like a can of red paint stuffed with raw ground beef, you wear out faster than you may think. You're gonna need time to recuperate.

For me, sometimes that means lazing around the house and watching old-school soaps or reading a sweet romance novel. Other times, I'll catch a matinee or go out on the town with my best friend Daphne. Occasionally, I'll take Howler to the dog park to run around. But that usually ends with the police being called.

Today, after yesterday's recording with the fatass who thought we were soulmates, I decide to go help with the church bake sale for my relaxing day off.

I know what you're thinking: *Church? She goes to church?!*

I do. Not because I think praying to the Almighty will gain me admittance to some paradise in the clouds alongside a bunch of canonized perverts. Church, for me, is a good palate cleanser. I sip fine wine and cognac on the regular, metaphorically speaking, so sometimes I need to consume a few dry crackers so I can taste again the sweetness of my daily routine. Plus, it's just fun listening to those old birds act like they know what's going on.

Upon waking, I take a warm shower and go about my morning necessaries. I dress in a pair of comfortable jeans and a sleeveless turtleneck that will allow me to get some sun on my arms, since the bake sale is outside the church's rec center. I put on a gold-colored necklace with a gold-colored cross that rests between my breasts above my shirt. (I don't know if the gold is real, but the local deacon who traded it to me said it was. What he traded it for was absurd; he'll probably need to visit a urologist to repair his 'good time'.) Then I pull my hair into a ponytail and perch glasses on my face. I don't need the glasses—they're not prescription—but they give me a kindly appearance that's endearing to the church ladies.

Men like the glasses too, the slugs. They see them as a weakness, as a sign that I'm quiet and bookish and easy to take advantage of. I like it that way.

Before leaving the house, I puree leftover organs with a cup of skim milk in my new commercial-grade blender, which I bought specifically for this purpose. I pour the concoction into Howler's food bowl just outside the backdoor. I sit on the back steps, petting his head as he laps up his breakfast. I love dogs and he's the best there is.

Sometimes I think I should train Howler to be an inside dog, but he's getting on up there in years. Plus, I really think he prefers being an outside dog, where he can chase squirrels and birds and bunnies. It's a spacious yard, giving him plenty of room to roam and sniff around. He's designated a whole little section for where he takes his shits.

The church is called First Assembly Church

of Grace. I have no idea where or when this first assembly took place—or who was involved in it—but it's a nondenominational domicile of worship. Though the regular parishioners would never admit it, they're pretty in line with the Baptist joint down the road, with all the Bible-thumping and railing against drinking and other unsavory behavior.

Easing my unassuming Buick into the First Assembly parking lot, I pull in next to a dirty pickup I know belongs to Martha's husband Frank. Martha is your typical middle-aged godly woman. Frank is your typical red-faced loudmouth, always talking about fishing and hunting trips he likely never went on.

Getting out of the Buick, I go over to the passenger side and take out the red velvet cake I baked two nights back and chilled in the fridge. It's what I always make for the bake sales; the other ladies have come to expect it. It's tasty, and it also makes it look like you're shitting blood if you eat too much of it.

"Well, there's Miss Sara!" an elderly blue-haired bird says from her seat behind the table, which is loaded with banana bread and brownies and pies and cakes and cobblers. There's even a handful of jars with labels claiming the contents to be tortilla soup, though it looks suspiciously like the vomit I spewed down the throat of the guy from last night's session. "We were beginning to think you wouldn't make it." The woman is wearing sunglasses that take up half her sagging face, yet she still feels the need to shade her eyes from the sun with one arthritic hand.

"Oh, I wouldn't miss this for the world, Lucille," I say, giving her a wink as I slide the red velvet cake amongst the spread. "You better have set aside one of your cherry pies for me."

"You know I did," Lucille says, winking back at me and pointing a gnarled finger beneath the table. Though, it looks more like she's pointing at her pelvic region, and for a split second I envision some naked and restrained slave man knelt between her legs, lapping at her crinkly cunt, getting long gray hairs stuck in his teeth, helpless and crying as he performs this deed.

There are five of them stationed behind the table in lawn chairs, all with similar permed hairstyles and similar rumpled flesh and baggy tits. Another two or three ladies poke in every few moments, pretending to help, asking how things are going.

One of these ladies is Belle Anderson, who, if I had to guess, is younger than me. As per her usual arrangement, she's jubilant beyond normal cheerful behavior, always showing her bleached pearly whites, laughing and talking with everyone about everything, running her hand through her thick hair repeatedly, walking with that sway in her hips that godly women should avoid. Belle is slender and big-breasted, and today she's prancing around in jeans and a t-shirt that looks to be painted on. She involves herself in every church function you could dream of, always huddling up close to the ballbags. The men, I mean.

With this hussy surrounded by women who are far beyond their prime, the rumor mill is predictably pumping out new accusations on the regular. She's slept with half the men in the congregation, according to some reports. Even the preacher's sixteen-year-old son, if each indictment is to be believed.

Belle purchases a pecan pie that Gretchen made and two of Martha's brownies. She comments how she wants to buy more but says she's trying to work on her figure. The old hens take Belle's money, say kind words, and wish her well as she goes back into the First Assembly rec center, where the preacher and deacon are supposedly going through items in the room used for storage. Belle says she's helping them "sift through the trash."

"The trash is going back inside," Alice Winkle says under her breath, and all the ladies of the bake sale share a good laugh, including me.

"I can't believe Preacher John lets a woman like that hang around," Martha says.

"That's men for you," Lucille says.

"They're all the same, even the good ones," Gretchen says.

"Not my Frank," Martha says.

All their gossip runs together now, just like their hair and flesh, no accusation distinguishable from the last.

"I saw her give Bill Streiber a hug after Sunday service. Pressed her bosom right up against him, like they were lovers."

"Carol Shaffer said she saw that woman drunk as a skunk at the Applebee's."

"She was hanging all over the high school principal at the homecoming game last fall."

"Word has it, there is a picture of Belle with her shirt off on the computer. No bra either. Showing it all."

"On what computer?"

"On the internet, you know. For everyone to see."

"She went to the rodeo with Chris Reinhart a few weeks ago. That man is seven years younger than her. Barely out of his teens. Since when is that okay?"

"God help that boy."

"God help 'em both."

"She's beyond help, I'm afraid. Satan's got ahold of her."

"Yes, ma'am."

"God bless."

"You know she was raised Catholic? That's how some of those Catholics are when they leave the Church. Some of 'em go good and some of 'em go crazy."

"Weren't you raised Catholic, Sara?"

"Sure was," I say. "The priest raped me when I was twelve."

Conversation dries up a bit after that comment. The bake sale goes well. Everything sells, including my red velvet cake. Preacher John, of all people, buys it. As I hand it to him, I whisper in his ear not to eat too much in one sitting because red velvet cake has been known to cause gastrointestinal bleeding.

He looks at me funny and chuckles nervously. His eyes shift to my breasts before he turns and walks away.

That Time of the Morning

When you're self-employed it's good to have multiple modes of income.

Occasionally, my monthly session will attract enough high-rolling viewers to cover my expenses for the month and then some. But I'm a girl who enjoys the finer things in life—weekly manicures, pedicures, facials, and deep tissue massages are a must for a chick on camera who needs to look her best. There are other not-so-cheap expenses, like the elevator I told you about. And I'm always adding to my tool and toy collection, to bring the audience a fresh experience every time I turn the camera on.

I buy more hand tools and electric saws from the hardware store than probably any construction company in town. If some new, fancy tool comes in, it's going home with me. From chainsaws to arc welders to your basic hammer, I've got it all. You'd be amazed how a souped-up power washer can spray the flesh right off someone's face. I even bought a hydraulic breaker—you know, for busting up concrete—and boy did that set me back.

Same goes for the local kink store. I've got every flogger and riding crop and whip and restraint and you-fucking-name-it they have. I'm such a good customer, I get a 10% discount on all products. They probably wonder what the hell I do with the hundreds of dildos and vibrators and sounding equipment I've bought. If they only knew.

Think about all the possibilities when you combine the hardware purchases with the kink store purchases! Let me tell you, it's amazing how deep a dildo will go when you attach it to the end of a twenty-foot auger. What really surprised *me* was how much shit spewed from the guy's mouth before the dildo finally made its appearance, growing out of his screaming mouth like a wobbling rubber bean sprout.

Speaking of shit, one of my alternate modes of income is visiting today for his bi-weekly. Because of the money I spend, these side sessions become necessary. Sure, I could crochet a scarf or do some other crafty nonsense and sell it on Etsy, but do you realize how long that takes? And then all the marketing and shipping involved to get your store off the ground? It's not worth it, trust me.

Besides, what I do for money when this particular client has an appointment, I do for free anyway.

I call him Toilet.

No-no! Don't skip ahead!

I realize you probably know what Toilet's kink is based on his name. But that doesn't mean you should hop over the details like cracks in the sidewalk. You asked about what I do and how I do it, so no skipping; stay the course.

My house is a modest three-bed, two-bath abode, with less square footage than you probably think. And one of the bathrooms is not a functional such room when it comes to relieving one's self. The master bath is normal, with a shower and bathtub, along with a spacious countertop and the required toilet.

But the guest bath in the hallway has a shower, a small sink with very little counter space, no tub, and no toilet. Where the toilet should be sitting, I've placed loose tiles that match the rest of the bathroom. (I considered epoxying the tiles over the plumbing hole and the rest of the affected area, but you never know how long a client will stick with you; I could patch up the floor today only to find out he can't afford to continue his sessions.)

The doorbell rings promptly at ten in the morning—Toilet is always right on time.

I'm outfitted in only my plush lavender

robe, as the client wishes. I pull the belt tight around my waist as I approach the door, adjusting my ponytail as I glance through the peephole. It's him alright.

Unlocking the two bolts, the doorknob lock, and the chain, I swing the door inward and smile wryly at him. He's thin and only about five-five, a small man of Asian origin, Japanese maybe, dressed in the business casual required for his accounting job. He's shy and rarely looks me in the eyes. Right now, as he holds the leather briefcase he always has, his dark eyes stare down at my feet. My toenails are painted lavender to match the robe.

"Hello there, Toilet," I say.

He nods without lifting his head.

"I've been waiting for you, you know. I could have done this two hours ago, but I held it just for you, you porcelain-wannabe bitch." I don't say this with anger in my voice, but sweetly erotic.

He flashes a brief smile, then it's gone as he

nods again, still gazing down.

"Well, get where you're supposed to be, Toilet, before I make a mess all over the floor."

Stepping aside, he shuffles past me, his subtle cologne catching my nose. He has more in his briefcase, I know, along with his usual soap and shampoo.

Toilet looks over his shoulder at me as he heads toward the hallway. His eyes touch mine and his head quickly whips back forward.

I close and lock the door, then walk slowly toward the hall, sliding my feet on the clean hardwood, twirling the tongue of my robe as I go. The hallway is dark when I turn into its mouth, all except the line of yellow light beneath the closed bathroom door. I lean against the wall next to the door, crossing my arms.

My lower abdomen grumbles uneasily.

There is an uncomfortable pressure down there.

"Hurry up in there, Toilet," I say, wrapping my knuckles lightly on the door. "I've been holding it all fucking morning."

There are quick, nervous movements from behind the door. Nervous breathing too. Then he falls quiet.

"Okay, Miss Sara," he says, his voice shaking.

"That's Mistress Sara to you," I say, grasping the doorknob, "that is, if toilets could talk."

I push the door open and stand there on the cusp with my arms crossed. Toilet is crouched where any standard commode would be. He's naked, his clothing folded neatly and stacked at the other end of the counter, his briefcase on the floor beneath. Due to his small stature and flexibility, Toilet is able to squat down very low, his feet and bare ass both resting flat against the tiles, his arms wrapped about his shins, his knees level with his shoulders. And his head is tilted back, his mouth like an O.

Smiling, I step forward and pull open a drawer beneath the countertop, then pull out the mouth spreader. It's a simple object, consisting of an adjustable black leather band, with stainless steel claws at either end. It's already set to Toilet's size, so I bend over him without a word and hook one claw inside his right cheek, then pull the leather belt around the back of his neck, stretching it until I'm able to snag the left side, pulling his open mouth into a gaping hole.

"There we are," I say, "my Toilet is fixed. Comfy?"

Toilet nods, his wet eyes blinking open, reflecting light from above.

"I don't give a fuck if you're comfy, Toilet. Don't answer me. Toilets don't respond. They don't *communicate*. Toilets exist for one reason and one reason only: to catch and swallow human waste. That's why *you* exist! To catch and swallow my waste! Understand?"

He almost nods again. Almost. His head wavers slightly, but he catches himself.

"Good," I say, standing up straight now, undoing the robe and sliding it from my shoulders, tossing it nonchalantly across the counter.

Toilet's eyes quiver, wanting to cut my direction and see my nakedness, to see my hips and full breasts and the short cropping of blonde pubic hair. But he knows better. I've trained him well. I have no doubt he opens his eyes once I start though.

I wasn't lying when I said I'd been holding it all morning. My belly hurts on account of it. I'm a little lactose intolerant, you see. Knowing Toilet would be here today, I deviated massively from my typical diet, which is mostly chicken salads, fruit/granola mixtures, and the occasional cheat day of chocolates and popcorn. Last night though: cheesy beef nachos, cheesy jalapeno poppers, a slice of cheesecake, and a tall glass of milk.

Honestly, I'm amazed I didn't shit the bed during the night.

Every step I've taken this morning has been a struggle of sphincter strength.

Now, I can feel it pushing to get out.

I turn around, lowering myself, like one does when sitting on the conventional toilet. Only, I do so slowly, steadying myself with one arm on the counter. Toilet, being a small Asian man in his daily life, isn't as sturdy as the shitter you get at Home Depot. So, I'm careful. My ass presses gently against his face, and very sedately I transfer my weight from my legs, until finally, Toilet is supporting all of me.

Then I let loose. No straining or grunting necessary.

I'd lined up my asshole perfectly with his cavernous maw. But it fills quick. Usually, he swallows with sufficient swiftness to ensure his mouth doesn't overflow with my excrement. Today is different. My lactose-ladened dinner—did I mention I also had a milkshake?—has resulted in a BM of explosive proportions.

Toilet is doing something he hasn't done previously: he's struggling. He's gagging and coughing. He's still swallowing, mind you, but he wasn't ready for this. It's probably a good thing the milk has made my stool soft, with even a few liquid spurts. If I was shitting a typical log this fast and furious, Toilet would probably choke to death.

As it is, he battles through to the end.

After only a few minutes, I've expelled everything from my rectum I can manage.

Sighing relief, I lean forward, unrolling some toilet paper and folding it sufficiently to my needs. Leaning further off Toilet's face, I wipe, feeling the wetness of it. Inspecting the used TP, I note today's stool is a lighter shade than most days. From the cheese, obviously. I deposit the wad of toilet paper into Toilet's mouth. His gullet does its work, swallowing it down. I wipe a few more times, until I'm satisfied with my cleanliness, and send it all into Toilet's waiting face. He has tears in his eyes.

I wash my hands and leave the bathroom without comment. Toilet spends the next thirty-two minutes cleaning up. It's agreed, as part of his bi-weekly session, that he can use the shower.

For taking a shit and allowing a small, strange Asian man to take a shower in my house, I make five-hundred bucks. As he leaves, he tips me another two-hundred and says today's session was the best yet.

Choices, Choices

Picking who will be the star of your recorded session, if you choose to involve yourself in this profession, is a tricky task.

Unlike men, we can't just knock someone over the head and throw them over our shoulder and dump them in the trunk for later use. Men are brutes, you see; they're not clever. They seek out the vulnerable and weak. You don't see a five-two man picking on a six-one woman, do you? Of course not. You certainly don't see a man raring back to lay knuckles on a trans woman, because that bastard knows he might be spitting his teeth into the dirt before things are settled.

They bully women because they can, because some spur of evolution decided men needed to be bigger, stronger, and faster. Meaner too, don't forget that. They have natural aggression written into their DNA the way dogs have sniffing each other's asses written into theirs. Some social anthropologists will say that aggressiveness exists as a protective measure, so men will stand up and fight to defend their family, allowing them to live and their bloodline to carry on.

I guess it's just a fluke when a man's aggression is used to slap his six-month-old infant girl so hard that her neck breaks. I guess it's a fluke when the same man's aggression is used to beat his wife within an inch of her life and rape her while she lay there crying for her deceased baby.

But enough about my failed marriage.

What I'm getting at is, we ladies don't have the natural strength and aggression like men. We can't just go snatch up whomever we please. And don't go watching these movies with the 'strong female lead' and think that shit's reality.

Just because Scarlet Johannson and Gal Gadot are kicking all kinds of ass on the silver screen, doesn't mean they can actually wield those talents in the real world. Gal, at least, had military training, so maybe she could hold her own for a little bit, but Scarlet? The average Joe Pencil Neck could knock her no-talent ass silly in three seconds flat, then drag her home by the hair and have his way with her.

Us women, we must be clever.

That doesn't mean you have to seek out those short, puny fellas, like Toilet. I've brought all sizes down to the basement for prime time, from tall and skinny to short and fat to musclebound meathead. You just have to go about it the right way.

Play the part they want—that's the first step. Be the vulnerable sweet piece of ass they're looking for. Be ditzy and bimboish. Act like you know fuck-all about football and jackshit about fishing and not a goddamn thing about his favorite books or movies.

But I'm getting ahead of myself.

First, you have to pick the dumb bastard.

Now, I know it's all the rage these days to find your 'special someone' online, whether through one of those hook-up apps or social media or even a dating website. But that's not ideal, for obvious reasons. You don't want your digital footprint stamped all over the laptops of dickheads who have gone missing.

So, get around town. Alone. Don't mix your search with your valuable friend time; that could muddy the waters. Go to coffee shops and department stores if you're looking for one of those hipster types. You know them, the guys who wear jeans tighter than a yoga instructor's yoga pants. They wear awkward glasses they believe make them appear edgy and quirky and unique, even though every fucking one of them wears the same stupid awkward glasses. They all stink faintly of espresso, IPA beer, and baby powder.

If you're looking for the country type of man who gets his hands dirty for a living, try the hardware store or, even better, the feed store. The bait shop too, if the season is right for fishing. Be careful though, these types tend to be heavier in the midsection than the rest (except for those 600-pound disability recipients who haven't left the house in three years). The big country boys are harder to take down, is what I'm saying. And sometimes they come armed. But if you play a little Hank Williams and pop the top on a Coors Light, you'll have those rednecks fawning like Pepe' Le Pew over a painted cat.

Want an unemployed pothead? Check the most run-down convenience store in town, one that used to be a gas station but no longer is, the type of joint that peddles almost solely in lottery tickets, Newports, and malt liquor. The guys you're looking for will come straight to you, asking to bum a cigarette.

If you're looking for the ultra-religious type, church functions on any day but Sunday are good. Feign any kind of helplessness and those uptight bible-thumpers will shuffle your way faster than you can say 'Bless me, Father, for I have sinned.'

If you want it to be easy, go to the cheapest pub in town, the one where the winos and deadbeat dads vomit their paychecks into the barkeep's register. This is a good option if you're not the most attractive lass—beer goggles are real.

The grocery store is another good one. My last star, as a matter of fact, I found in a grocery store parking lot. I made one innocent move, and that sucker was mine.

Today, though, I'm going to the gym. Like I said, I've had my way with the meatheads before. Watch how it's done.

Real Work Sucks, and So Do Men

You're probably wondering how and why I got into this profession.

A smart lady like myself, without a college degree, I could probably make a hell of a living as a secretary or waitress, am I right? No. Perhaps if I worked overtime at one of those, I could afford an efficiency apartment on the bad side of town.

But I could go to school for six weeks or so and become a certified nurse aide, right? Sure, if I want to spend my days wiping asses and changing bedsheets for just a fraction over minimum wage.

But, if traditional unskilled labor jobs won't do, I could become one of those flesh merchants on OnlyFans, right? Right. Have you seen what the *average* skank makes on that site? It ain't much. And I'm an average-looking gal. The only way a chick like me makes money on OnlyFans is by doing something crazy, like sticking wine bottles or baseball bats in her ass. That's a big no thanks.

But, Sara, you may say, *you already do crazy shit*.

Correct. But not to myself. I'll smash some balls or cut off a dick or shit down a guy's throat, but nothing and no one touches *me* or goes inside *me* unless I want it to. No amount of money changes that. So your average porn sites wouldn't work for me, I'm afraid.

But I haven't been in this line of work forever.

I worked in sales for seven years at a giant chain electronics store. You know the one with the big, obnoxious yellow sign? That's the one I worked at. Seven years of my life spent at that shithole. Not that it was all bad; the knowledge of camera equipment and streaming I acquired while there has proved invaluable.

But the coworkers, the customers, and the goddamn managers—almost all bull-headed, know-it-all, useless men, of course—nearly drove me crazy over those seven years. I thought I would never get out of there. But I did, and I still remember my last day . . .

"Yo, can I get someone to give me the lowdown on these tablets?"

"What would you like to know?" I said, approaching the two young men slowly, my hands clasped behind my back. They were mid-twenties, probably, same as I was at the time. They were tattooed and pierced and wearing saggy britches. "Are you wanting something for gaming or streaming or something else?"

The one who asked the question, with his spikey green hair, turned and looked at his buddy, as if he just heard one hell of a joke. Then he turned back to me. "You know about computers, lady?"

"Quite a lot, actually," I said, stoic-faced, not at all surprised by the punk's assumption that I probably didn't know Hewlett Packard from Hawk Tuah. Usually, it was the men in their forties and fifties who found it hard to believe a lass like myself knew anything beyond how to scroll through Instagram; younger men typically gave me the benefit of the doubt. I continued: "What kind of operating system do you prefer? Windows, Mac, ChromeOS? You looking for something with a lot of RAM? What about storage space? Do you need a laptop you can use on the go, something with plenty of battery life?"

Green Spikes stared at me, bemused, then looked back at his friend. In unison, they burst out laughing.

"What's so funny?" I said, crossing my arms over my chest.

"Nothing," Green Spikes said, waving his

hand at me, clutching his stomach with his other hand, trying to control his laughter, "I just ain't never seen a chick that know shit about computers." The giggles resumed between the two.

"There is nothing inherently masculine *or* feminine involved with knowing about computers," I said, turning red. "It's pretty fucking sexist to think that way, you know?"

Their chortles tapered off as their eyes met mine.

"I know a shit tone about guns too. Is there something wrong with that? I can take a disassembled Glock 19, reassemble it, load it, pump fifteen rounds into your gut, and disassemble it again in less than a minute. Can you do that, asshole?"

This was true. I can still do it. And have.

"Okay then," Green Spikes said, then looked over his shoulder at his friend, "we going to Circuit City now. I ain't dealing with this crazy-ass bitch."

"Excuse me?" I said, but the two of them were already moving for the door, each giving me wild-eyed stares as they passed me. "Yeah, well—"

"What was that about, Sara?"

It was my shift manager, Hank. He was your typical electronics store shift manager: balding, a belly that hung over his belt like excess dough in a muffin pan, below average height, below average IQ, and probably below average dick size. Hank was always watching me, waiting for me to do something he didn't approve of. I also caught him looking down my shirt on multiple occasions, when I bent down to grab something for a customer.

"Did you just run off those customers?" he said, placing his hands on his hips the way he always did.

"Hank," I said through gritted teeth, leaning close to him so as not to make a scene, "those two dickheads just called me a crazy bitch."

"Oh, is that right? Why would they do that,

Sara? Did you say something?"

"Uh, yeah, I asked them what they were looking for. What the *fuck* do you think?"

"That's it? And they responded by calling you a bitch?"

"No, they responded by pulling their little cocks out and telling me to get on my knees," I said, turning red. "I'm tired of putting up with the bullshit, Hank."

"Okay, okay," he said, holding his hands up. "We can talk about it after your shift. We need to discuss your sales numbers anyway. They've been really down lately."

"Oh, my numbers are down?" I said, grasping my shirt collar. "Am I not showing the customers enough cleavage?" I tore open the top three buttons of my shirt, exposing my bust. "Is that it, Hank? Will I get more sales now?"

"Jesus Christ, cover yourself up," Hank said, holding his hands out toward me like he was blocking anyone from viewing me, his head whipping around nervously. Several bewildered customers looked on. "Just take the rest of the day off, Sara. Come in tomorrow at noon and we'll talk things out with Glen, okay?"

"Glen?" I said, getting in Hank's face now, making him back up a step or three. "That pervert of a general manager has been trying to get in my pants for years. He was going to promote me to shift manager instead of you, Hank, but I refused to participate in a gangbang at the company Christmas party."

"Alright, Sara, that's enough. Just go!" Looking frantically around him, Hank said, "So sorry for this, folks!"

"Sorry? Ha! You weren't sorry when you sent dick pics to my sixteen-year-old sister."

"That is not true! Folks, that is not true! Disgruntled employee! Can we get someone to escort Sara out of here, please? Tyler, Mitch, one of you, please?"

"Don't send your minions after me, you pedo piece of shit. I know my way out." With that, I ripped through the rest of my buttons and threw my shirt on the floor, leaving me with only a white bra on my top half. Spinning away from Hank, I stormed for the exit.

There was an elderly man walking slowly through the entrance as I left. I informed him he needed to stop staring at my tits unless he wanted me to remove his shriveled nutsack with a pocketknife and feed it up his ass. He promptly looked away.

Sure enough, Hank's wife left him when she found pedophile files on his computer. He killed himself not long after.

Obviously, I never went back to that job. I needed something to make ends meet. Something I would enjoy, too. I would not be a weak woman in a man's world any longer. I pegged my first bitch boy about a week later. He paid me a hundred bucks to prolapse his rectum with a rubber cock.

I've never looked back.

The Palace of Mirrors and Grunters

What a weird place to spend one's time.

Palace Fitness—where grown men and women pay ridiculous monthly sums to lift heavy things and trot on treadmills, as if paying a onetime fee for weights of their own and jogging around the neighborhood are out of the question—is my current location.

As I push through the door, I'm smacked in the face by the scent of sweaty armpits, unwashed linens, and copious amounts of disinfectant. R&B music plays softly overhead, interrupted frequently by weights being dropped dramatically back into place, metal against metal—an ear-busting noise if there ever was one.

"Hey, there, I don't think I've seen you here before, not before," a young guy says, coming around the counter near the door, ahead of the gym floor. He wears a polo shirt, but it's way too tight. I can actually see his nipples through the fabric. He's also spent way too much time in a tanning bed, like a high school chick from the 90s. "You looking to sign up for a membership, a new membership? It's only—"

"Not yet," I say. "I'd like to try the place out first, to see if I like it."

"Oh, no problem, no problem, cool, cool," he says, nodding enthusiastically, rubbing his hands together like he's warming them over a fire. "I'll just need a form of ID to sign you in. Just a form of ID." I guess he likes repeating himself. He holds up a finger-thumb combination to demonstrate the shape of a driver license, in case I'm too dimwitted to comprehend.

"Great," I say, taking a small leather money

clip from the side pocket of my yoga pants, removing the fake ID and handing it to him.

"Wonderful, wonderful," he says, taking it and trotting back to the desk. "Great day for a workout. I'll have this back to you in a jiff, in just a jiff."

He starts explaining that I can only come exercise this once without payment, that I'll have to get a membership from now on, and then he starts explaining some of the safety rules as he's entering my information into his computer. But I've heard it all before. This is my third time coming to Palace Fitness. Third ID I've used. Third style and color of hair—I wore a black wig with bangs this time, and I must say it looks pretty good with my eye color and skin tone.

"Do you have any questions?" he asks, handing me back the fake ID, smiling absurdly wide, putting on full display a crooked tooth right there in front.

"No, thank you," I say, and he pushes some button behind the desk that allows me to walk through the gate into the gym without a membership card.

I know exactly where I'm going: the steppers. The handful of steppers at Palace Fitness are stationed to where the exercisers upon them can see people in the free weights section to the front left and people in the cable weights section to the front right, both areas where men predominately do their thing.

Today is no exception. As I mount the stepper and get started at a slow pace, I see there are about a dozen men, along with two ladies, in the weight-lifting sections before me.

There are two chest press machines situated side by side and both of them are occupied by young men, neither of whom are using the damn things. They're both looking down at their phones. One of them is wearing an absurdly tight Under Armour shirt. Not only can I make out this guy's nipples, I can also see the cropping of acne across his chest. The other man is wearing basketball shorts and a regular t-shirt, but also a sweatband around his head. Unless he's expecting the AC to go on the fritz during his stay, I don't think he's in much danger of sweating.

Oh wait! He's placing his phone in his lap and grasping the handles of the chest press and . . . releasing the handles to once more pick up his phone. The hussy on the other end must have sent him another text.

Neither of these two will do.

About half the guys in the gym are staring at their phones, getting absolutely nothing accomplished. That goes for one of the chicks I see too.

This one moron—wearing extremely baggy sweats that, honestly, look like they could snag on something and cause all sorts of issues in a gym—is standing in front of the dumbbell racks and holding *two* phones, one in each hand. He's looking at the phone in his right hand, and the phone in his left looks all sad and forgotten. He also has big headphones over his ears and he's bouncing his head to some unheard music.

He looks my way briefly, but I offer no wink to suggest I'm interested.

The dumbass with the sweatband gets up from the chest press without having done a single exercise, at least not while I've been here, which is a good five minutes now. He deposits his cellphone in his pocket, then pulls three disinfectant wipes from the dispenser nearby. He proceeds to cleanse the chest press machine as if it were a piece of equipment in an operating room, like any trace of bacteria must be found and destroyed, lest open surgical wounds become purulent pits of infection.

The other half of the men—the ones not looking at their phones—are universally staring at themselves in the mirrors as they do various exercises. Like most gyms these days, Palace Fitness has its walls completely wrapped in mirrors. To promote this sort of behavior, I suppose.

One skinny dipshit has a bench pulled right

up to the mirror, and he is doing curls with what looks like either a ten or fifteen-pound dumbbell—pretty fucking lightweight. Yet, his eyes are staring intently at the mirror, at his bicep, watching each flex like it's a once-in-a-lifetime work of art. He's gritting his teeth too, as if the ten-pounder is really doing a number on his noodle arm.

Now, I'm not too picky when it comes to physical attributes, but if I can easily kick the dude's ass in hand-to-hand combat without breaking a sweat, he's not my type.

Someone drops a barbell back onto a rack from too high, causing a metallic ringing crack to pierce my skull, making my ears ring, drawing my attention away from the ten-pound curler. Only now do I realize I was smiling at the scrawny lad.

At the bench press, where the loud clanking sound came from, a muscular man is rising to a standing position, swinging his arms about and grunting like a gorilla. He's wearing the remnants of a t-shirt. It would barely pass as a snot rag or a cloth diaper. Mister Muscles has clearly taken a pair of scissors to his shirt. Either that or someone attacked him with a katana but only sliced his shirt.

The sleeves are gone. Where they should be are only giant holes that go almost all the way down to the bottom of the garment. His mountainous shoulders are exposed to the clavicle, where the thin piece of fabric of the shirt's collar clings to life. Across the front of this tattered shirt are the letters A-C-K-E-R. The other letters are butchered from existence, but judging by the color combination, I'm guessing it was a Green Bay Packers shirt before its untimely demise.

"Yeah!" Mister Muscles says way too damn loud, drawing the eyes of others.

Walking to a mirror, he flexes one arm, then the other, then both at the same time. He does several different flex poses. You know, the way they do. I can't tell for sure from this distance, but his body appears to be completely hairless.

His rippled flesh glistens with sweat. Flex on, flex off. Flex on, flex off.

Holding his arms away from his body, Mister Muscles waltzes over to the cable tower. The guy bouncing his head to the music in his headphones is in this general area, so Mister Muscles points to the cable tower and raises his eyebrows in question to Mister Headphones. Mister Headphones shakes his head and Mister Muscles smiles and nods and sways his shoulders as he continues to the machine.

Pulling the pin from one of the top weights, he replaces it near the bottom of the stack, making it a very heavy lift. Then he grasps the straight bar attached to the cable just above his head. He starts breathing out in heaves, grunting, and saying "do it" over and over. Then he performs a successful triceps pushdown, screaming and grunting and turning all red-faced the whole way down, his veins bulging in his neck and temples, his arms bulging, sweat raining down on the floor mats around him.

This one, I tell you, this one is mine.

Snagging a tool such as this is as easy as catching an ant in a blob of honey. Even for a gal like me—who, as I've suggested previously, is no peak Demi Moore—getting this man is duck soup. I have a nice enough rack, sure, but that's not what it's about for self-loving tool bags like Mister Muscles here. He'd bed down with a chick twice as ugly, three times as hefty, four times as hairy, and ten times more stinky than me.

Why?

Because it's about *him* and the attention he's receiving. Not about you. Not about any individual woman. It's about attention and numbers for Mister Muscle. Yes, numbers. He would take two anorexic geriatrics over one supermodel, I assure you. As long as the geriatrics had enough strength in their old bones to show him some attention.

I turn the stepper machine off and slowly dismount it, my thighs aching slightly from the exercise. In the mirror across the way, I can see my face is flushed red. That's good. Not that I need the help with this type but being flushed offers an extra illusion of desire. I walk slowly toward the cable tower and Mister Muscles, as he grunts and yells and makes a scene.

"Are you, like, a competitive bodybuilder or something?" I say, sounding ditzy, leaning on a rack of weights not far away.

Mister Muscles, just now noticing me, releases the straight bar mid-pushdown, causing the bar to shoot up to the top of the tower and the weights to go crashing down to their place of rest, making a sound that should have shattered a few mirrors. The noise appears not to phase Mister Muscles, though myself and everyone else in Palace Fitness winces in unison.

"Hi there," he says in a voice I can tell he's forcing to be deeper than his usual. "I lift a little bit, ya know." His hands are on his hips now and he's flexing his arms as he talks to me. "But I don't compete, even though I'd probably win."

"I bet you would," I say. "I don't think I've

ever seen anyone as strong as you." I'm laying it on thick. I could stick my pinky in my mouth to look absurdly sheepish, but decide against it.

"Oh yeah? Well . . ." He trails off, looking down at himself, flexing some more, trying unsuccessfully to hide a smile.

"I bet you know how to handle a woman, huh?" I say, going straight for the kill. "With those strong arms. Those . . . strong hands." I bite my lip.

Mister Muscles looks quickly up at me, grinning broadly. "Of course I do. You know it." He's still flexing.

"I don't really like gyms. Do you think, if you don't mind, you could give me a private lesson sometime? Like, at my house?"

"Of course, baby," he says, and now pulls a cellphone from the pocket of his shorts. "Gimme your digits and we'll set something up."

Instead of my phone number, I enter my profile name for an app that allows for private, untraceable conversations. When I'm done, I hand the phone back to him and he takes it and deposits it back into his pocket without looking.

"Cool, cool," Mister Muscles says. Then he informs me he has a name other than Mister Muscles. "I'm Grant, by the way. And I can come by your house any time, you know, to *show you* a few things. Just not Tuesday, because that's when I get waxed. Makes my skin kinda red and tender, you know?"

"Of course," I say. "My name is Megan."

"Like that chick?" Grant says.

I have no idea what chick he is referring to. Before I can ask for clarification, some other tool shows up.

"Hey, what's up, bro? Who's the lady friend?"

They could almost be twins if not for the different skin tones and hair colors. The new arrival—Mister Flex, I'll call him—is equally muscled and free of body hair. He too is fond of shirts that could barely pass for a fat lady's thong. The only real difference between Grant and Mister Flex is that Mister Flex has a flat-billed ballcap on his head, turned around backward. It has, I notice as he turns to eye himself in the mirror, a '69' stitched above the bill.

"Yo, what up bro?" Grant says, holding his hand up to Mister Flex. They slap hands and snap in unison. "Yo, I was just talkin' with this chick—yo, what's your name again?"

"Aileen," I say, crossing my arms beneath my breasts, pushing them up as I watch these two dolts interact.

"Right," Grant says. "Anyway, bro, I'm gonna give her private lessons."

"Private lessons?" Mister Flex says, raising his eyebrow, smiling but looking confused, his eyes going from Grant to me then back to Grant. "Lessons of what, bro? You play piano or something?"

"Jesus, no, bro! I'm showing her how to work out and whatnot, you know? You know, she—"

"I invited him over to my house to fuck me, if you want to know the truth of it," I interrupt, pushing up on my breasts some more. "You can come too, if you like. Three's not a crowd in my book. What's your name, big guy?"

Grant and Mister Flex look at each other wide-eyed, then back to me. Mister Flex talks, sounding stupid: "You mean me?"

I sigh, smiling. "Of course I mean you, Mister Flex."

"Oh, um, my name is Billy Wickaninnish."

"Lord, let's stick with Billy," I say. "It's settled then. Hit me up tonight, Grant." I point to his pocket where his phone is. "We'll set a date." Then I point at the bro from another ho. "You come too, Billy boy."

Turning on my heel, I head for the door, unable to contain my smile. This will be fun. Way more fun than when I was nineteen and cornered at the gym by five men and forced to be the central attraction of a late-night gangrape.

Fuck those grunting gym rats.

"What was your name again?" one of them hollers from behind.

"Dorothea," I say over my shoulder as I exit Palace Fitness.

Drama at the Pharmacy

The key to a good live session is preparation.

You wouldn't go to war without training the troops, would you? You wouldn't attempt a backflip on the balance beam without tons of practice on the mat, right? You wouldn't bed down with your crush without first inquiring about which buttons to lick and which to avoid, true?

Wait, scratch that last one—particularly you men. You dipshits don't ask and certainly don't listen. Not with that veiny worm doing all the thinking for you.

But what I'm saying is, planning is crucial. You don't want to march your fella—or two *fellas*, in this case—into your dungeon and then have to figure out what to do with them. So, since leaving the gym, I've been mulling over exactly what I plan to do for my next livestream.

As I said before, I've got a wide variety of *things* already, so I don't need to fill a grocery cart with pain-inflicting tools or rectum-destroying dildos. But I do need to grab a few items from the pharmacy.

The automatic doors slide open and a rush of cool AC washes over me as I stride inside. There's a pink-haired emo girl at the checkout counter, but she ignores me as I walk toward the rear of the store, where the pharmacy portion is.

Once there, I wait patiently behind two other customers as they pick up their orders. Then I approach the counter and tell the pharmacy tech whose prescriptions I'm there to receive. She types something in her computer then goes back to some shelves and sifts through things back there.

When she emerges again, she has four small, white paper sacks clasped in her hand, each one with medication information stapled to the outside. She asks me the birthdate of the individual whom I'm obtaining medication for, because one of these medications is a controlled substance. I relay the individual's birthdate promptly, and the pharmacy tech nods and rings up the total. I pay in cash and am on my way.

Before leaving, I decide to get a cream soda from one of the many coolers along the wall. Cream soda is the best soda. It's what my dad used to buy me when I was a little kid. Cream soda makes me think of sunny days and swimming pools and fresh-cut lawns and The Wallflowers playing on the radio and catching my brother fucking my best friend. In *my* bed, of all the places he could have chosen.

There is a young man getting some groceries at the checkout counter, so I get in line several steps behind him. He's tall and clean-shaven, not terrible-looking but not model material either, thin-framed and sporting one of those permed hairdos that make his head look like broccoli. He's jacking his jaw at the emo girl as she scans his items and drops them lazily into plastic sacks.

"Where did you get your piercing work done?" he says, running his hand through his curls nervously. He's smitten. "I mean, I'm just curious. They did a good job. The tat work too, um, yeah, they did good work on your arms. That one of the gnome with the gun in his mouth, that's dope."

The emo girl stops scanning and looks up at the young man, scowling at him. As you're probably picturing, she's got a nose ring, two eyebrow rings, a stud in each cheek, and a variety of rings in each ear. Her arms are heavily tattooed and there is, indeed, a short mythical creature holding a revolver in his mouth, his eyes wide with terror, and brains and blood exploding out from behind his funny little hat. But that's not a gnome.

"That's not a gnome," Emo Girl snaps. "That's Grumpy, of the Seven Little Dwarfs. You know him?"

"Uh, yes," the young man stammers, "of course I do. From *Snow*—"

"Grumpy is the fucking dickhead that said all females are poison!"

Emo Girl stares up at him as if this explains something. The young man is staring down at her, perplexed, like the gears in his brain are grinding in an attempt to remember if he wronged this girl at some place and time. I, too, am a bit confused. The emo girl is doing a piss-poor job of getting her point across. If indeed there is a point. But, hey, I'm entertained.

"Okay," the young man says, after a full thirty-second stare down. His voice is barely audible as he continues: "But, uh, I'll go ahead and pay for that stuff when you're done scanning it."

Emo Girl breaks out of her stare and starts

back to angrily running his items across the laser. Now, instead of dropping his things into bags, she's slamming them into the bags, all while saying she's 'tired of this shit' and 'people need to show some fucking respect' and the young man needs to 'keep his dick in his goddamn pants.'

When she's done scanning and rings him up, Broccoli Head fumbles with then drops his debit card as he pulls it from his wallet. He has trouble picking it up off the floor, muttering 'shit' three times as he tries to come up with it. When he does, he actually holds it up, as if to demonstrate to Emo Girl he's capable of lifting such things from the carpet. Then he nearly drops the card again as he holds it over the card reader. Sweat collects at his temples as he types in his PIN. Apparently, he gets it right, because then Emo Girl prints out a mile-long receipt and hands it to the loverboy without comment. He snatches the plastic bags and walks quickly to the exit, red-faced.

I approach the checkout counter with a smile and set the cream soda down.

"Men, right?" Emo Girl says, shaking her head.

"Right," I say, though I'm unsure what the question means.

"That's why we choose the bear," she says as she scans my cream soda. "Want this in a bag?"

"What's that?" I say.

"Do you want your drink in a bag?"

"Oh, no. But the first part: what about a bear?"

"Oh," she chuckles, handing the cream soda to me, "you know what they say: between a man and bear, us women, we choose the bear."

I don't have the slightest idea what she's talking about. I'm nodding, taking a step toward the door, intent on letting my confusion remain when curiosity gets the better of me.

"I'm sorry, maybe I've missed something. Could you explain what women are choosing a bear to do?"

"Not on social media much, huh?" Emo Girl says, sitting down on a little stool behind the counter and crossing her arms. It's only now I realize she's chewing gum, smacking on it annoyingly. "Someone posed the question on TikTok—or maybe it was Insta first, I don't know—asking if you were walking in the woods alone if you would rather come across a man or a bear. And all the women are saying they'd rather come across a bear. Because fuck men."

I look at her for a moment, considering this. Then I ask, "Is it a certain kind of bear? Like a black bear or panda or what?"

"I don't know, just a bear. Doesn't matter."

"So it could be a grizzly bear?" I raise an eyebrow.

"Yeah, why not? Fuckin' better than a man."

I take a deep breath and rub my forehead before continuing. "What kind of man are we talking about? A heavyweight boxer jacked up on steroids and testosterone?"

"No-no-no," she says, waving her hands at me. "That's just it: you don't know what kind of man you'll come across. Could be a rapist. Could be a murderer. Could be fuckin' Jeffery Dahmer."

I don't bother explaining that Dahmer only killed men and boys, not women. A role model if there ever was one.

"Have you seen the men these days?" I say, pointing toward the door Broccoli Head recently exited through. "Most of them are fucking pussies. They spend their hours playing video games, getting perms, and jerking off to PornHub. If you came across that idiot in the woods, I think you're safe. In fact, he may ask you for directions on how to get the fuck *out* of the woods. 90% of men are just like that dumbass walking out of here with his tail between his legs. And you would rather have a bear? 100% of bears are bears. They could rip you in half from your cunt to your pink hair."

There is silence for a few seconds, then Emo Girl mutters, "I'm still choosing the fuckin' bear."

"Grow up, bitch," I snap. "Any man steps in front of me in the woods, I'm fucking his ass up. No questions asked. The problem with women like you is that you all think you're too goddamn weak to defend yourselves. Grow some fucking balls."

I storm out of the pharmacy without waiting for her to say anything in return. Part of me wants to take Emo Girl under my wing and show her how it's done. Would she still choose the goddamn bear if she knew she was perfectly capable of luring a man into the woods and tying him to a tree of his own accord, then whipping him with razor wire until every inch of his flesh drips into the leaves? I know she could do it because that was how I did it for one of my early sessions.

Maybe another time I'll reach out to her. Maybe she'll be game. But I've still got plans to work on.

As I get to my car, I notice the vehicle beside mine, an older model Honda Civic, has a baby and a beagle in the backseat. The Civic is not running and the windows are rolled up. And it's pretty warm outside. The baby is beet-red and crying, and the dog looks sad and tired, its tongue hanging out lazily.

Alarmed, I unlock my car and pull the crowbar from beneath the front seat. Looking around, I don't see anyone else that could help. I've never had to smash open a car window before, so I'm not sure how hard to hit it. Deciding to go full-on, I swing for the front passenger window, and it shatters instantly, raining into the seat.

I reach into the car, to the back door, and unlock it. Tossing the crowbar back into my car, I open the Civic's backdoor and scoop the beagle into my arms.

"Were you hot, little girl?" I say in a sweet voice. "Who left you in there?"

I snuggle and kiss her and scratch under her chin. Once her tail is wagging, I set her down on the pavement and send her on her way. I bump the Civic's back door with my booty, closing it. Then I drive home to feed Howler his dinner.

Yes, I left the baby in the backseat. It was a boy.

Hanging With My Bestie

Daphne is a hospice nurse, which means every patient she comes in contact with is on the brink of death. It also means she works weird hours, like weekends and nights and whenever else some breathing corpse is getting closer to that not-breathing stage. Even so, I find the time to hang out with her.

She gets bored and lonely when she's couped up inside an empty house with only the dying to keep her company. Sometimes family is around, Daphne has explained, hanging all over the frail individual, sobbing through every shallow, gasping breath their loved one makes.

But oftentimes, the closest the bereaved come to their moribund mawmaw is a cringe-inducing facetime call. Sometimes not even that happens.

So Daphne gets bored. She invites me over. And I bring a bottle of wine to sip with her while the *other's* heart draws nearer its last beat.

This time she's at an older home on the outskirts of town, probably a quarter mile from the nearest neighbor. It's a two-story affair and was undoubtedly a nice place fifty or sixty years ago. But now paint flakes from sun-faded boards, and shutters hang askew. There is even a broken second-floor window, surely the doing of some brazenfaced young boy with a rock.

Parking my car in the gravel driveway alongside Daphne's car, I get out and sling the purse containing the wine over my shoulder. I take in the house, a stiff breeze sweeping around me, the setting sun peering through the woods nearby. First the gravel crunches beneath my footfalls, then the boards of the porch steps whine, followed by the aching moans of the porch itself as I come to the front door. I have my doubts that the doorbell works, but I press it anyway and am pleased to hear a gentle, almost elegant ring.

After a series of creaking steps from inside, the front door opens and there stands my best bud. Daphne is short and solid, with fiery red hair and a chest that is sure to cause her back problems down the road. Even the baggy scrub top she's wearing is insufficient to conceal her considerable bust.

"Hey, girl!" she squeals as the door swings inward, holding her arms out to me.

"Hey!" I say back as we embrace. "How you been, Miss Daphne?"

"Oh, swell, Miss Sara. How about you?"

"Shit, the only things that could make life any better would be endless orgasms and a lifetime supply of chocolate pie."

"Tell me about it, girl. Come on in!" She waves me in as she spins around on her socks. (Daphne frequently kicks her crocks off when there's no family around.) "I was getting bored out of my ever-loving mind. No TV here, and I can't get the radio to work. I have my phone, of course, but the battery is getting low so I can't sit there and piddle too much."

"Well then," I say, bowing slightly even though her back is to me as she walks deeper into the house, "I am at your service to entertain and enthrall."

"Oh, hush! You know I love your company." She looks over her shoulder and waves her hand again. "Come on, his room is back here."

His. Of course it's a him. That's why the family isn't here. He was probably a prick to them for seventy or eighty years, and now he's lying in bed with no one to look after him except a stranger with big tits and a bottle of morphine in her pocket. Could be worse, I guess.

I follow Daphne down a short hallway and then hang a left across from a staircase, bringing us into what would have been a nice day room many moons ago, with plenty of room to stretch one's legs and an expansive view of the yard and woods to the west. Now, however, it survives only as a miniature healthcare facility, with stacks of folded linens, adult diapers, and as-yet-unused biohazard bags all over the place. There's an empty urinal on one end table and a dozen or more pill bottles on a TV-free entertainment center.

"Welcome to my home away from home," Daphne says, spinning around with her arms outstretched. "And this young fella is Marcel Rupert Chapman. Say hi to my friend Sara, Marcel!"

I raise an eyebrow as I look toward the old man. Most people on hospice aren't morbidly obese—impending death has robbed them of their tissue—but Marcel Rupert Chapman is like a blob of putty laying there in his Medicare-provided electric hospital bed. His hair is thick and ghost white, and his eyes are the lightest blue. But they're vacant, looking not at me or Daphne or any one thing. They stare into oblivion.

"Severe dementia and newly discovered stage four brain cancer," Daphne says matter-of-factly. "If he greets you with anything other than a burp or fart, I'd consider it a miracle."

"Delightful," I say, and I'm actually thankful for his inability to communicate. "Don't suppose your patient is gracious enough to provide two hot, young ladies with wine glasses?"

I pull the wine bottle from my purse, holding it up the way a waiter at a fine restaurant is want to do. Daphne smiles out of one corner of her mouth, tilting her head to examine the bottle, knowing damn well she can't tell a petite sirah from a fucking Mike's Hard Lemonade.

"Oh, I'm sure there's some wine glasses in the kitchen somewhere," she says, nodding her head toward the door. "But like everything else in this house, they're probably covered in dust and dead deer flies. Are you saying I need to do dishes before sipping a little wine, Sara?"

"Nah, I got us covered."

I pull two red plastic cups from my purse, setting them in an empty spot among the clutter on the entertainment system. I use a fold-out bottle opener to pull the cork. (I used the same bottle opener to gouge out a man's left eye a couple years back; it's been washed thoroughly since then, however.) Without bothering to let the wine breathe, I pour each of us generous helpings.

"For the lady of the house," I say, handing Daphne her cup with a slight bow.

"Awe, thank you, fair wench," Daphne says, mirroring my bow.

"Fair wench?" I say, and we both burst out laughing.

So we sip wine and talk nonsense like ladies do when in good company. With Mister Chapman's brain turned to disease-ridden mush, we pretty much act like he's not there at all. Occasionally, he moans and grimaces. But only when he shudders does Daphne pause the conversation to drop sublingual morphine under the fat bastard's tongue.

He shudders, Daphne explains, when he's *really* in pain. Also, when he shudders, he ripples. He's not wearing a hospital gown, though there are plenty of them, and his blanket is pulled up only just below his belly, causing me to witness his entire naked torso in the event I glance that direction. And let me tell you, he ripples when he shudders, like a fucking vat of vanilla custard riding in a wagon on the Oregon Trail.

We sit on the couch and talk favorite dessert recipes and favorite grocery stores and the best way to get a stain out of the carpet. Daphne tells me about this new South Korean reality TV show she's watching. I tell her a North Korean reality show would be far more entertaining. She agrees, though neither of us expand on the thought. We talk about dogs and romance novels and the new Taylor Swift song and the best bang for your buck vibrators on the market.

"About out of wine," I say, dispensing the

last of the bottle into our two cups, barely a mouthful for each of us.

"That's okay," Daphne says, sipping from hers. "I can't be all smashed when my relief gets here at midnight."

"Round-the-clock care for this vegetable, huh?" I say, pointing a thumb at the geezer. "Why not stick his ass in a nursing home?"

"Hell if I know. His daughter lives in France somewhere, hasn't seen him in years, but insists he wouldn't want to be anywhere except in his own house."

"Hmm," I say, and my head slowly swivels to where I'm gazing upon the geriatric blob with a raised eyebrow.

I doubt he would know whether he was in his house, in a nursing home, or in a goddamn landfill. The thought of Marcel Rupert Chapman lying naked amongst a landscape of garbage bags—with all the rotting food and soiled diapers and used condoms—makes me chuckle. I'm a shit drinker; half a bottle has gone to my head.

"I've got to pee," Daphne says, getting up from the couch and stretching her back and grimacing.

"That back of yours wouldn't hurt if you weren't so top-heavy," I say, winking at her and laughing. I'm no lesbian. I don't lick the lower lips. But I'd be lying if I said I never thought about burying my face in Daphne's tits.

She just rolls her eyes. "You good here if I go to the bathroom?"

"Yep," I say, nodding slowly, feeling the wine swimming around in my head.

Daphne walks to the day room entryway, then turns around. "You sure you're good in here alone with Marcel?"

"I got it, girl," I say, throwing her a thumbs up.

"Okay, I'll be back," she says as she disappears around the corner.

Letting out a deep breath, rasberrying my lips, I get up and stretch. I've been here less than two hours, but it feels like I've been sinking into the couch for days. The heaviness of my eyes is only exceeded by the heaviness of my feet as I take a few steps into the middle of the room. For a brief second, I worry perhaps I drugged myself with the concoction I normally brew up for men. But that's ridiculous: I opened the wine tonight and mixed it with nothing. I just can't hold alcohol worth a fuck.

In an attempt to come out of my stupor, I roam around the room looking at the pictures on the walls, all of them in need of a good dusting. There is a black and white photograph of three young men standing at the edge of a lake, all of them shirtless and slender, smiling like the world will never end. If one of the men is Marcel, I can't tell which it would be. There is an old color photograph of Marcel in what was likely his mid-forties, with thick brown hair and a bushy mustache that's since been shaved away. He's big at this point in his life, but not obese. There are several paintings on the wall, some of bird hunters and some of fishermen and one of Jesus Christ with his head lowered in prayer.

Moving along, I come to the dresser, with all the gowns and hazardous materials bags piled on it. Pulling open the top drawer without thinking, I scrunch my face at what I'm suddenly seeing. Photographs—dozens of them. Some have Marcel Rupert Chapman in them, at various ages, and some don't. What all the pictures contain, though, are children.

Naked children.

Doing things children should not be doing.

There, in one, is Marcel, his hair greyed and his belly looming, with his small, purple cock clutched in his fist, tight as if he's trying to keep it hard. Standing before him with a worried, disgusted look on her face is a young girl. Eight or nine, maybe. With blonde hair, just like my own.

Shoving the drawer closed, shaking, furious, turning red, I spin around to look at the oversized puddle of wrinkled flesh. He's breathing lightly, his chest barely rising, his eyes cracked only half open, blank, vacant, gone. Behind those eyes, cancer and dementia or not, is the brain of a vile, downright evil man. The worst kind of man. Never caught, apparently. Never made to pay for his deeds. Never delivered his just desserts.

Until today.

There's a handful of walking canes leaning against the end table beside his electric bed. I grab the thickest, feeling the smooth, finished wood in my hands. Stepping up to the bed, I raise the cane over my head, the hook end just barely missing the fan blades. My eyes are wide with fury. His eyes never see the oncoming horror.

The first hit shatters his nose, sending blood spurting from each nostril, turning Marcel's relatively straight beak into one that resembles a question mark. But that's only hit one. I quickly raise the cane again as the fat slob coughs but otherwise shows no discomfort. I swing downward, crashing this time into his mouth, knocking out many of what remained of his teeth.

The assault becomes a blur. The cane smashes into his face repeatedly, breaking his orbital bones and jellying one eye, opening up lacerations on his cheeks and under his eyes and across his forehead. I'm hitting him so hard and so many times that before long, the impacts are making wet, squishy smacking sounds. His face becomes a bloody pulp resembling a raw pork roast more than a human being.

I come down once more and the cane snaps in half, the blood-drenched hook end tumbling over the other side of the bed and skittering across the floor. Left in my hands is half a walking cane with a sharp splintered end.

Daphne finally emerges from her trip to the bathroom after I've stabbed Marcel Rupert Chapman in the dick and nuts about a dozen times.

"What the fuck, Sara?!"

My back is to her, so I slowly turn my head to peer over my shoulder. She's standing in the entryway with her arms outstretched, her eyes wide with shock, one long strand of out-of-place red hair cutting her face into halves.

Turning back, I look down at the cane-half in my hand. It's painted crimson, and pieces of unidentifiable flesh cling to its splinters. The rubber ferrule at the end of the cane is the only part not dripping gore, though there is one blood splatter there too. Similarly, my hands are soaked red and my forearms look like an abstract painting. My clothes, of course, were not spared desecration. But blood comes out pretty easy in the wash.

Lifting the cane one more time, I drive the sharp end into Marcel Rupert Chapman's jelly-like abdomen, hitting his cavernous belly button straight on. When my hand leaves the slick wood, the cane piece is jutting from his stomach like a stake in a vampire's heart.

"Sorry," I say as I turn around to face Daphne.

She's standing in the same place, though

her arms have dropped to her sides in a defeated manner. "Fuck, Sara, I knew I shouldn't have left you alone with him."

"Daph, he's a piece of shit," I say, pointing a finger at his ruined face. "Seriously, a fucking pedophile. The worst. Check the top dra—"

"You could have at least shot him up with insulin like you did the last guy. No mess with that. Goddammit. I'm gonna have to stop inviting you over when I'm working, girl."

"No, don't say that," I say, and tears are forming in my eyes. Daphne is my bestie. It would truly hurt my heart if she stopped asking me to keep her company.

"My relief will be here in just over two hours," she says, holding a hand toward the bed as if to say *So, what the fuck are we doing about that giant fucking mess?*

"Should we burn the house down?" I say, shrugging.

We do, indeed, burn the house down.

Fetch Me an Orgasm

You want to be loose for your live session. You want to be focused but not too much. And you don't want desire creeping into the equation. That's why you need to get your nut the night before.

I know what you're thinking: it's *men*, not women, who need a toe-curling orgasm before they can think clearly. First off, even after blowing their load in a rag or into the toilet or all over some poor bitch's face, they still can't think clearly. It's not in their nature.

For women, though, a good orgasm *does* help us. We're sexual creatures. I know it, you know it, everyone knows it. We try to pretend it's not the case, by acting delicate and shy and uninterested. By playing hard-to-get. But the point is always to be *gotten* in the end, right, girls? You just want that goddamn man to do things correctly before giving it up. It's not our fault God made every one of them lying, lazy oafs. We're just as libidinous as men, if not more so. We simply know how to control our lustful cravings when we're not getting what we want.

Typically.

Desire can be a funny thing, even for us strong ladies. So, if you're bringing a hunky man or two into your lair tomorrow for a session, then get laid tonight.

The screen door creaks as I push it open, then guide it back into place behind me. The stars are brilliant tonight, with no clouds to hide their beauty. The moon is crescent and slender, seeming to peek from behind a blind. The breeze is cool on my naked body. Descending the concrete steps, my bare feet touch down in the recently manicured St. Augustine.

The backyard is dark. Neither the back

porch light nor the light next to my shed in the western corner of the yard is on. Only the stars, the sliver of moon, and the soft glow of the strip mall not too far away offer light within the boundaries of my wooden fence. Scanning the yard, I see no movement, not even the stirring of a wind-blown branch on my fig trees.

"Howler," I say, squatting down, clapping my hands gently. "Come here, boy."

Howler is an early sleeper. Unless he hears neighborhood kids playing in the road, which makes him bark incessantly, or someone is popping firecrackers, which makes him go insane, then he'll be laid up against the shed or the fence somewhere, catching Zs. He has a doghouse not far from the backdoor, but he never uses it unless it's raining. And it has to be pouring down at that.

"Howler," I say, crouching down to all fours, crawling further into the yard, my eyes adjusting to the lowlight. "Time to wake up, big boy. Time to play with Mama."

Queen Boss Slay

There is a rustling ahead of me and to the right, by the fence. I see him moving, a dark shadowy mass in the night. Howler is a big dog, even as far as big dogs are concerned. He's up on all fours now and I see him looking at me, his head cocked to the side, the universal sign a dog is trying to figure out what the hell the owner is saying or wanting.

"Come here, Howler!" I say with the jubilation of a little girl, clapping my hands together. "Come on, good boy!"

Howler moves forward cautiously. I got onto him for barking at a cat earlier. He was even trying to jump the fence, probably in hopes of mauling the poor thing. But I don't put up with that anymore. He killed a whole litter of kittens a few months ago—ripped them to pieces, tearing their poor little heads off their poor little bodies. The mama cat had given birth behind the shed. Not a good idea on her part.

Anyway, I gave Howler a good lashing with a stick when I found out what he'd been up to. It was the first time I'd ever done that to a dog, and hopefully the last. But I snap at him every time he even growls in the direction of a cat since that day. He'll learn. The good scolding he received earlier has made him timid tonight.

So, I switch tactics. He likes it when I'm direct anyway.

"Who's my good doggo?" I say, turning around on all fours, my feet and ass facing Howler. "Who's my big, strong, good doggo?" Looking over my shoulder at him, I spread my legs slightly, gliding a hand across my inner thigh until my fingers trace the gentle flesh of my vulva. "You want to make Mama happy, don't you, Howler, my good doggo?"

He doesn't hesitate now. He knows exactly what I want.

He bounds across the yard, and I stick ass up and out, arching my back, closing my eyes.

Howler is on top of me and *in* me in seconds, his large, hard shaft pushing deep into my wetness, filling me. He thrusts hard and fast, an animalistic fuck. And I clutch at the grass and scream out, letting him take me, ravish me, have his way with me. He claws at my back and sides, grunting excitedly, his drool dribbling across my skin.

He's quick. Less than ten good hard thrusts bring him to climax, and I feel his doggy goo shooting into me. My body has grown accustomed to his swiftness, and an orgasm quickly blooms from my loins too. Slamming my ass back against him, my toes and fingers digging through the grass into the dirt, the orgasm explodes, causing my whole body to tense and quiver.

When it's over, Howler pulls out of me, sniffs and licks briefly at the spunk that's dripped from my pussy to the grass, then lays down beside me, falling almost instantly asleep. Rolling to my back, I scoot close to him and watch the stars for a time. The night is cool and nice.

Howler's name used to be Doug Martin. He was a computer programmer for one of those big software companies when we first met. Come October, we'll have been married four years. When you find a good one, ladies, make sure you collar that sucker. It takes a lot of training, though.

Two Hunky Visitors

Nine out of ten of my live sessions go off without a hitch. It's been eleven smooth sessions in a row now, so I'm due some trouble, but maybe not. I've gotten so good at this, with all the planning and such, that maybe putting me in a basement dungeon with lots of leather and sharp instruments and power tools, is like handing Leonardo da Vinci a blank canvas, a paintbrush and paint, and a basic-looking chick in need of a portrait.

But you don't want to be overly confident—trust me on that. You don't want to be the self-assured queen bitch who ends up the victim in her own live session.

The last time things went sideways, I'd given the lucky fella a paralytic that didn't paralyze him as long as required for my livestream. He wasn't restrained, on account of he shouldn't have been able to move. But I'd just severed off his cock and balls with a fillet knife—a recurring theme in my act—when that bastard came out of his paralysis like he'd only been taking a catnap. He sprang up from the operating table, kneeing me in the nose in the process, and started running around the basement waving his arms, with blood pouring from his cockless crotch and toothless mouth. (I'd pulled his teeth before whipping out the knife.) Needless to say, I had to fire up the chainsaw and put it to good use or that fucker would have killed me and gotten away.

At least I got it on video. That night paid *damn* good.

Even so, I'm not in the business of asking for trouble. I want everything to go as planned, with no chance of me losing my head. Since today's live session involves two musclebound buffoons who can probably be as violent as they are stupid, I'm taking extra precautions.

The first precaution you want to make—particularly if you live in a neighborhood, as I do—is to schedule your session during the day. There are two reasons for this: one, you want most of your clientele to be overseas viewers, because the more complex the legalities of the whole thing, the better; two, a guy or two showing up to your house in the middle of the day could mean anything, like perhaps they're just there to check the plumbing or help put together some furniture you ordered off Wayfair.

It's not conspicuous, is what I'm saying, to have someone show up during the day. But if you have some dude driving down your road in the middle of the night, blaring his hip hop and shining his headlights through everyone's windows as he navigates his way to your house, you'll have every nosey set of eyes in the neighborhood peaking from between the blinds to see what's going on.

You'll still have to watch out for the nosey neighbors, even during the day. My next-door neighbor, Miles, the Vietnam vet I told you about, was of the inquisitive variety. A little too inquisitive. I took care of him after catching him peeping in on me in the shower while choking his chicken. The police still have him listed as a missing person, last I checked, and they even issued a silver alert during those first few days. They'll never find him though; I diced him into pieces during a livestream, then divided him up into equal portions and mailed him to the five clients who watched that day. The cost of overseas refrigerated shipping for five heavy boxes was absurd.

Grant and Billy, the musclebound lunkheads from Palace Fitness, arrived three minutes late in the same car. (Good, because one car to dispose of is better than two.) I answered the door swathed in a black velvet robe, with my fishnet-clad legs visible just below the knees. Grant and Billy, wearing basketball shorts and tight t-shirts, were visibly excited, if their eyes and the twitching in their shorts meant anything. I fixed them each a gin and tonic, with a dash or four of my favorite sedative, a mix of Ambien and Ketamine, shaken not stirred. Then I told them I would be back in a jiffy, that I needed to slip into something nice. By the time I returned, all outfitted in leather and lace, they were slouched against each other, drooling all over themselves.

Thank Christ for the elevator in my hall closet. I guess it's true about muscle weighing more than fat because even getting Grant and Billy into the wheelchair I use to transport folks was a chore. But I got it done.

Now they're on the mattress, just rousing.

Yeah, I decided on the mattress this time. I don't use it much because things tend to get so messy, so the surgical table usually works best. But with these two strapping chaps, the surgical table would not have provided enough room.

Plus, I decided to be a backseat driver for this session. You'll see what I mean.

The mattress is a queen, just like me, and it's covered in a hot pink fitted sheet. It looks perfect against the glossy black tiles of my dungeon basement, with the pink wall backdrop my viewers are used to seeing, along with the stainless countertop with several instruments thereupon, within reach of the mattress.

Precaution number two was purchasing a couple coils of razor wire, which I encircled twice around both the mattress and stainless countertop. It only comes up about two feet, so one of the dolts could step over and certainly jump over, but it will cause a pause if they do try to escape. And usually, a pause is all I need to have the upper hand. Plus, I couldn't very well build a razor wire wall, which would obscure the scene for our viewers.

I have three top-quality cameras poised around the scene on tripods, each one connecting to the livestream when I press start.

Viewers can then take in the action from different angles. Or all three angles at once. I have my laptop ready on a stainless desktop, and I'll monitor the livestream and any requests that may come through from my clients. Sometimes they're quite active. Other times they're quiet and just like seeing what I come up with.

Grant and Billy are naked, splayed out across the mattress, their limbs entangled. Both of them appear to be fond of the full-body waxing experience because they're virtually hairless below the jugular.

Grant stirs first. He already has a hard-on, and his face, neck, and chest are flushed red. Which is to be expected when three-hundred milligrams of Viagra have been fed into your belly through a nasogastric tube. Yeah, that's a large dose. And yeah, I'm mildly surprised he didn't awaken as I shoved that tube in his nose down to his stomach. But the sedative cocktail was also a large dose.

I gave Grant the Viagra because he looked

to have a slightly larger penis, which is preferable for what I have planned. But I must say, revealing their combined endowment during the disrobing process was a disappointment. That tends to be the case for big guys.

Grant's moving around gets Billy to stir too, stretching his arms and groaning. Now is a good time to start, before they're fully awake and cognizant. Leaning over my laptop, I see four clients are waiting for the livestream to begin. More will come along as things get going. I hit Go Live, then move quickly in front of the nearest camera, snagging my flogger off the desktop.

"Hello, all you lusty ladies and worthless, shit-eating men," I say, twirling the flogger around, letting its leather tassels slap my breasts. "Welcome to another thrilling session with your favorite domme! The baddest BDSM bitch in the land! The top twat of torture! The mortal enemy to all men, even those of you who are watching. Especially you!" I point at the camera with a long, sharp nail. "Welcome, friends and foes, to Queen Boss Slay!"

Queen Boss Slays

Even before I'm done with the brief opening monologue, I hear some dings from my laptop, indicating I've received tips. These, without question, are from the male viewers. Despite my open disgust and constant insults of their dick-swinging sex, they still regularly make up three-quarters of my viewers. Go figure.

"Today, I offer you a special treat. It's not only *one* pitiful penis possessor you'll witness meet his maker, but two. That's right, ladies and pricks, I've acquired two strapping studs with nothing better to do than lift heavy things and admire themselves in the mirror. Not bad bodies on these fucks, I must say." I peer over my shoulder as I say this, as if looking at them with desire.

"But they're flawed like all others, aren't they, ladies? Arrogant, narcissistic, self-loving ballsacks that take advantage of women at every turn. Men like this have been trampling on strong women since we were all living in caves. Well, as always, I'm slicing off a little of that historical supremacy for the finer sex. For the women!"

Gritting my teeth, I whip my flogger at the camera, then spin around toward the mattress and the razor wire and the two hapless hunks at the center. Standing just on the other side of the wire, I put my fists on my hips, smiling down at them. Grant and Billy are still groggy, but coming out of it, becoming aware that something is going on they're not sure they want to be a part of.

"What is this?" Grant says, rubbing crusties from his eyes.

"Welcome to the land of the living, boys," I

say, cutting my eyes at the camera across the way. "It looks like Grant here is ready to go. He's got himself a little boner. Emphasis on *little*!"

Grant looks down at his package and covers himself with his hands, at the same time trying to stand and protest his predicament. Billy is doing the same thing, attempting to rise. But the sedatives haven't completely abated, so they're clumsy and both of them nearly topple into the razor wire.

"Easy, boys," I say, slapping the flogger at them, smacking Billy across the face gently and whipping at Grant's cock-covering hands. "Just rest on the mattress for a minute. You're not going anywhere."

"What is this?" Grant says again.

"What's going on?" Billy says, his voice and face identical to that of his partner in toolship.

"Is this being taped?" Grant says, noticing the cameras with wide-eyed horror.

"Taped?" I say, looking to one camera with a chuckle. "Fuck no. What century do you think we live in? This is livestreamed."

"What?!" they both exclaim at once, each of them once more trying to get to their feet, while simultaneously covering their privates.

"That's right," I say, and now I move off-camera to the seat by the stainless desk. Once seated, I set the flogger aside and lift my third precaution, the AR-15 that was leaning against the desk, tricked out with a Vortex red dot and Banish suppressor. I hold it up at a comfortable position but don't point it at them yet. "You're being livestreamed, and you're doing everything I say."

The laptop is dinging with tips. Six viewers. Now seven.

"Alright, Grant," I say, leveling the AR at him, "to start with, fuck your buddy Billy there. And Billy, don't try to resist. I've made it relatively easy for you to start with—I slathered your asshole with nitroglycerin rectal ointment, which loosens your muscles back there, making things more accessible for your friend. Basically, you can't clench your butthole out of this situation."

"This is ridiculous!" Grant screams. "I'm not doing it! Let us go!"

He's rising wobbly-legged to his feet when I quickly raise the AR, putting the red dot where I want it, and pull the trigger.

Grant's left ear disappears with the pop of the gunshot. The suppressor doesn't silence the shot, the way movies make you believe, but it keeps the noise from rattling the speakers of my viewers' devices. Grant's sudden screams are louder than the gunshot. The pink wall beyond him is spattered with his blood. His hand hovers over the ragged spot where his ear was.

"Stop screaming and start fucking," I say, waggling the barrel at both of them. "I'm a crack shot, as you can see, so don't make me shoot something you'll miss more than one lousy ear."

"Please, don't do this," Billy says, tears forming in his eyes and quickly tumbling down his cheeks.

"Billy boy, get your muscular ass in the ready position before I shoot off that pretty nose of yours. Or that pathetic dick." I'm not lying on either count: he has a pretty nose for a man and a sad dick that's shriveled to nothing with fear.

Slowly, shaking, Billy puts his hands on the mattress, on all fours now, the doggystyle position.

"Arch your back," I say harshly.

To my surprise, he does arch his back. I thought for sure I would have to send a .223 round zipping past his face before he'd comply. His firm man rump is pointing directly at Grant now. But Grant is avoiding eye contact with the brown eye. He's looking glassy-eyed at me instead, his dick still standing at attention. That Viagra works great.

More dings of tips coming in. Up to ten viewers now. That's pretty good.

"Alright, Grant," I say, pointing at Billy's ass with the AR, "get to work. Don't act like it's your first time."

"I've never fucked a guy in the ass," he says, his voice breaking, blood dripping down his left arm from his ear. "I'm no fag."

"You got something against gays, Grant? That's not very nice. You've stuck your dick in a hole before, right? Well, there's a hole. Put your dick in it before I shoot the tip off." I raise the AR to my shoulder so he knows I'm serious.

"Okay," he squeaks, tears flowing from him now too.

He inches forward on his knees, his cock leading the way. His trembling hands take hold of Billy's ass cheeks, spreading them apart. Both men look scared shitless, and I'll be damned if I can tell which one more so. Grant's dick hovers before the butthole for a second, less than a centimeter away. I see him about to spit on the tip for lubrication.

"No spit necessary," I say, wagging the AR in the negative. "The ointment I used makes him easy enough to penetrate."

Grant looks at me with pleading eyes, on

the verge of saying something.

"Keep your mouth shut and get after it," I say.

And so he does. Turning his attention back to his exercise partner's asshole, he pushes slowly forward, into him, the ointment-loosened rectum seeming to suck the cock into it. Billy, for his part, screeches at the air, his hands clutching at the pink sheet, his face going red, his eyes clenching shut, as if he's in terrible agony. But he's being dramatic, in my opinion. Anal sex isn't that fucking bad. I should know.

Grant is clutching at his buddy's ass the same way Billy is clutching the sheet, like he's both afraid it will get away and afraid it will come any closer. He has stopped pushing forward, despite an inch or two of cock still visible between his body and Billy's.

"Back and forth, Grant," I say. "Jesus Christ, you know how sex works. Fuck the hole."

He's actively crying—sobbing even, with snot bubbles and everything—as he starts the reluctant in and out motion. Not to be outdone, Billy screams even louder, spilling tears all over the sheets.

It's hysterical. The laptop is dinging with tips and requests. One request suggests I let them both fuck me, which is not fucking happening. What livestream do they think they're watching? I type a polite message to the clients stating I won't be taking requests on this one, that they should sit back and enjoy the show, that I've got it covered.

Before I'm even done typing, Grant is yelling through gritted teeth, veins protruding from his temple and neck, his body red and sweaty and jerking. Is he cumming?

"Did you just orgasm, Grant?" I say through laughter. "Did you just cum in your chum?"

Grant is sobbing again, looking super sad and humiliated, taking one hand away from his friend's ass to wipe tears away. Billy isn't screaming anymore, but his sobs are great. The fucking motion has stopped. They're frozen on the mattress like two secret lovers caught in the act by an unknowing spouse.

"Go ahead, pull out," I say. "Let's see what kind of mess you made."

It doesn't take him as long to pull out as it did to push in. Sure enough, his pussy penetrator is dripping with white goo, thanks to a man's poot shoot. A blob of the jizz farts out of Billy's ass and splats to the sheet.

"Can we go now?" Grant sputters through sobs.

This is an absurd request, of course. "So much for stamina, huh, Grant? Have you ever pleased a woman in your life?"

"Can we please go?" Billy says, trying to come out of his doggystyle position.

"Fuck no," I say. "Stay on all fours like a good bitch." I tap the AR with a fingernail to remind them who is in charge. "Now, Grant, on the other side of the mattress, you'll notice a stainless table with some goodies on it."

His head slowly swivels to the table and his

eyes widen, seeing it for the first time.

"You've probably noticed, Grant," I continue, "that your legs feel numb. That's because I shot them up with an assload of lidocaine while you were unconscious. You should thank me. Because your legs being numb will make this next part a lot easier."

I'm about to finish up explaining what Grant's next task is when he snatches something off the stainless table, then quickly spins back around, hurling the something in my direction, saying "Fuck you, bitch!" as it tumbles end over end toward me.

It's the meat cleaver. A damned expensive sucker too. And this bastard is tossing it at me like a cheap throwing knife, like something that can get a little bent and broken without damaging the value.

Thankfully for my face, Grant's aim is off. He was no pitcher in high school, I gather. It pings off the wall behind me and clatters to the floor. At the same time, I raise the AR-15, peering through the glass, putting the red dot on the right hand that just flung the cleaver. Grant is bringing it back up, his body turning, his face in a twisted scowl. He's going for another weapon, I realize. But he's too late. With his hand outstretched over the table, I pull the trigger.

The bullet tears through his upper palm and rips through his middle finger, nearly severing it, but leaving a single band of flesh between the finger and the rest of his hand. Screaming, Grant pulls his arm back, and the finger swings around by that length of tissue like a tetherball.

It's only now that I notice Billy rising to his feet, crouching and about to leap over the razor wire, at which point I'll be in significantly more danger. But I'm quick with the rifle. Aiming low, I take out his left ankle. Billy—screaming, though not as loud as when he was getting fucked in the ass—topples into the razor wire.

More dings from the laptop. This is adding up to be a fantastic session already.

Billy is all tangled in the razor wire, the

razors slicing into his flesh in a dozen or more places. From my angle, I can see his ballsack is one of the areas caught by the sharp metal; it's lacerated and bleeding profusely. His right cheek is also caught, and as he tries pulling his head away, the wire lifts with him, digging several razors deeper into his body. Billy's screams and whimpers are delicious.

I let them both wail and bleed for a few minutes—Grant falling back to his knees, staring in horror at his ruined hand, and Billy all mixed up in the razor wire and making things worse with every movement. Once I've had enough, I call to them.

"Alright, boys, that's enough crying," I say. "Let's get back down to business before the lidocaine in Grant's legs wears off."

"Please!" Grant whines.

"Shut up," I say, then point the AR at his hand. "To start with, go ahead and rip off your dangling finger and shove it in Billy's ass. It's his now. As a matter of fact, stick your whole fucked up hand in his ass."

Grant stares at me with wide-eyed horror, his trembling mouth hanging open.

"Go ahead, that ointment I applied shouldn't make it too difficult. Finger first. Rip it off."

"Noooo!" Billy screams, all wrapped up in razor wire. It's comical that he's actually in a better position to be fucked in the ass now than when he was kneeling on the mattress. His bubble butt is about the only thing on his body not crisscrossed with sharp wire.

"Get after it, Grant," I say, "unless you want me pulling this trigger again. Put the finger in first."

Through sniffles and sobs that would be impressive for the most irritable toddler, Grant takes hold of his dangling middle finger with the still-dandy fingers of his left hand. Then, closing his eyes, he jerks the digit away like a dad pulling out a kid's loose tooth with a string. Several inches of skin tear away from the back of his hand, which must be incredibly painful, but he gets the job done.

"Good," I say, offering him a thumbs up. "Now up the bunghole with it."

"Don't do it," Billy whimpers to Grant over his shoulder, a razor tearing at his face with the movement. He's really off his rocker if he thinks Grant is going to listen to *him* instead of the person holding the gun.

At an annoyingly leisurely speed, Grant inserts the finger into his buddy's behind. It disappears like the mole in a Whac-A-Mole arcade game.

"Now your hand," I say.

Grant sobs but doesn't protest. I guess he's finally figured out how fruitless that is. He starts inching his still intact left hand toward Billy's bum.

"The hand with the hole in it, dipshit," I say sternly as a cluster of dings continue on the laptop.

So in goes the hand with four digits instead

of five. They both whine in pain during the insertion. It takes longer than I'd hoped for him to get it in. Billy must have a nice tight asshole, despite the ointment. Grant buries his hand up to the wrist. I wonder if he can feel the finger in there or any shit. No shit came out on his dick, which was kind of disappointing.

I tell Grant to curl his hand into a fist in his buddy's butt and start punching the colon like it's a speed bag. As he cries and says 'no' repeatedly, he makes punching motions inside Billy's ass. Billy screams bloody murder, getting all cut up on the outside. But I'm getting bored with the whole ordeal. And the dings have slowed.

"Alright, enough of that," I say. "Out with the hand."

At a snail's pace, like he's sad to do it, Grant removes his four-fingered hand from the ass. At least it has shit on it. Clumpy, smears of dark stool decorate his fingers and knuckles and the place where his middle finger once was. It looks like hard poo, the type from eating too much protein and not drinking enough water, the kind that can be a real pain to shit out.

Looking past Grant to the table, I consider what to make him use. The cleaver would have been my first choice, but it's dented and on the floor behind me, and I'm not turning my back on the boys. My next choice is probably the better choice anyway.

"Grant, you see that electric knife on the table there? Grab it. All you have to do is turn the switch on."

"P-p-please, just let me g-g-go," he says, looking at me with pitiful eyes, blood running down the left side of his face and dripping from his shit-covered right hand. "Let m-me g-g-go." Funny how he's not so concerned about Billy being let go.

"Fuck no," I say, waggling the AR once more. "Grab the electric knife. This is where you can thank me for shooting your leg full of lidocaine. You can thank my dog, Howler, too. Without his prescriptions for Viagra, lidocaine, Ambien, and nitroglycerine rectal ointment, all of this would have been significantly more difficult."

None of this seems to reach Grant's one good ear. He just stares at me.

"The electric knife, fuckface!" I yell, raising the rifle to my shoulder. "Get it before I shoot your balls off!"

It's crazy how easy an electric knife makes it to cut through flesh. Seriously. The cleaver or a good chef's knife have more of an appeal visually, but you can't beat the efficiency of an electric knife. It makes things so damn easy, especially for the unwilling participant. All he has to do is touch the flesh—no pressure or sawing necessary.

Grant picks it up with his good hand and, to my surprise, turns it on without prompting.

"Great," I say, "now, fillet off strips of flesh from your legs and feed it into Billy's ass."

"What?!" Grant screams, holding the buzzing knife out like a soiled diaper.

"You heard me. Don't worry, it shouldn't hurt much. Unless you wait too long and the lidocaine wears off."

This gets him reluctantly moving. I'm mildly surprised he doesn't take the knife to his neck. He has to know he's going to die at this point. He's been getting his way for so long, he's not quite sure how to react when he's been bested. Same with Billy. That fuck isn't making a peep. He's accepted his fate of having flesh crammed up his ass while snuggling up in razor wire. My, how the mighty have fallen.

Grant eases the electric knife down on his left thigh and avulses a thin, short strip of skin, so thin it's translucent. I tell him to get a little meat before I butt fuck him with a bullet, so he shaves off a strip about the size of a slice of raw bacon. Blood streams down either side of his thigh as he silently sets the knife aside and pushes the wadded strip of meat into Billy's butthole.

The laptop dings away. Eighteen viewers

now.

I keep this going for a while. Grant carves up his thighs and calves like a chef carving up a turkey. Before long, there is very little skin left; only the reddish-pink of muscle beneath, still shapely from years of strenuous exercise, though tattered and bleeding from the knife. I make him fillet off the soles of his feet too. He goes a bit too deep on his right heel, and I can see the white of bone when the chunk falls away.

Every bit goes up Billy's ass. It's like the trick where clowns pile into a small car, except this is pieces of sawed-off human flesh going into a dude's rectum. Honestly, I'm impressed he hasn't shit it out. I'm curious if he's having to hold it in or if his bowels are just capable of taking it.

"You can stop now," I say after a reasonable amount of filleting and stuffing has gone on. "One last thing, Grant and Billy, I promise. Then it's over."

Neither of them responds. Grant sits there

staring at his shredded legs the way a kid looks at his snow cone after dropping it on a hot sidewalk. Billy just lays there, his eyes staring blankly in the direction of one of the cameras. If it weren't for the breathing, he would look dead.

The electric knife is still purring away in Grant's hand. This is good, because he still needs it.

"For this last act," I say, "you'll need to open up Billy's asshole a bit more. The ointment isn't enough, and all that cramming and stretching you've done isn't enough either."

"W-what?" Billy says, suddenly roused to the land of the living. "Please!" He moves about, only digging himself further into the wire.

"Grant, take that electric knife of yours and saw open his ass. Cut up and down and left and right, a few inches each way. Then saw a circle around it and pull out the pieces you cut. Got it?"

Billy is nonplussed over this one. He starts freaking out and really trying to get away, thoroughly slicing his flesh to bits in the razor wire. Lacerations everywhere. A big one opens up on his toned stomach, pouring blood out. Another is bleeding real bad on his neck and I'm wondering if it got his jugular vein. His ballsack is in fleshy ribbons and his little peter isn't looking much better. He keeps fighting, though, trying to get away.

At this point, I'm not convinced threatening him with the AR will do much good, so I just tell Grant to get after it. Like a good little puppy dog, he does exactly as I fucking said. He is gone mentally, I think.

He pushes the buzzing electric saw into Billy's gaping asshole, sawing down to the base of his balls. Blood spills out everywhere as Billy screams and flops about like a fish caught in some netting. Grant pulls out, changes the angle of the serrated edge, and cuts all the way to the top of his ass crack. Then he cuts left and right too, just as I said, tearing into the meaty portions of his toned rump. Grant attempts to draw a big circle around that but doesn't really succeed. It's a mangled mess. He saws and digs out meat and such, but it's not looking quite like I expected. And Billy keeps fighting like an uncooperative jerk. Eventually, I tell Grant to stop and turn off the knife, that the hole looks big enough.

Grant does as he's told, pulling the knife away, flicking the switch off. The whole contraption is covered in gore, as are Grant's arms and Billy's backside. He tosses the electric knife to the bed, then just sits there staring blankly at his work, at Billy's gaping ass and his own skinned lower half. He doesn't seem to feel upset about it at all. Just blah. Like he has just endured a really hard workout at the gym and needs to relax, maybe take a little nap.

Billy is moaning quietly, barely conscious by the sound of it. He's lost so much blood.

The laptop is dinging away. Dozens of dings.

"Grant," I say, standing up, holding the AR at the ready with both hands. "Oh, Grant."

He's slow, but his head swivels my way. Those eyes are blank. His brain has been broken by pain and fear and helplessness. By defeat he didn't think possible.

"Grant, put your whole head in Billy's ass. Once you've done that, eat everything in there. All the meat, all the shit, and lap up all the blood. Got it?"

Grant blinks, looking confused, thinking hard, like a five-year-old contemplating advanced physics. Then suddenly, his face clears and he almost smiles. He looks me in the eyes, and nods.

"Good," I say.

And he does what I told him.

He edges forward on skinless knees. He places his hands on the backs of Billy's thighs. And quite to my surprise and to the surprise of anyone watching, he practically dives in headfirst. You would think he was trying to headbutt Billy's coccyx. No slow descent—he rockets his head down there, and with a splat of gore and crunch of God knows what—fucking hell!—he's in there! I didn't think it was possible!

The laptop is rapid fire-dinging. They're machine-gunning me with tips.

Grant's neck is wiggling around in Billy's ass, presumably as he consumes his dinner. His hands are pulling at Billy's cut butt flaps, opening it as wide as possible, so he can get however deep he can get. Billy isn't responding at all now. Dead, I guess.

I let Grant go at it for a few minutes, then I tiptoe up to the edge of the razor wire. Smiling, I look over at the nearest camera and give my audience a wink. Leaning over behind Grant's nude body, still quivering as he munches down inside Billy, I push the barrel of the AR-15 gently into his asshole. He doesn't seem to notice. Then I crouch down a little, making sure the rifle is level with the boys. I look at the camera again, all smiles, and I pull the trigger.

I May Have Lied

That was by far my most successful session. I could take a few months off, honestly. Do a little traveling or something. But I won't. I enjoy what I do too much to take a break from it.

That's right, I enjoy it.

I might have fibbed to you about a few things along the way. I might have said some things that made you think this was all about revenge, that I'd been wronged so many times by so many men, that men as a whole deserved my wrath.

Well, not so much. Here's the truth of it:

You know how I said my dad raped me when I was six? Yeah, that never happened. My dad wouldn't hurt a fly. Never even spanked me growing up. Mom didn't spank me either. I was brought up in what you might call a pleasant upper-middle-class household. It was fine. My brother didn't even fuck my best friend, like I'd said. (I tried to get him to fuck her while she was passed out on Xanax I mixed in her ice cream, but he was too much of a nerd and pussy to even try.)

The priest that raped me when I was twelve? Nah, I made that up too. Father Josef was a kind enough fella. He prayed over me like I was the antichrist. My turn in the confessional was always a barnburner. Honestly, I'm surprised he never tried an exorcism.

The ex-husband of mine that killed my baby and beat and raped me? Hell, I was never married. Not until Howler, anyway. I wouldn't subject myself to some asshole I couldn't control.

Hank from my previous job, who sent dick pics to my sister and was caught with pedo files on his computer? First off, I don't have a sister. The pedo files, yes, those were found on his computer. I put them there. And then he killed himself—that part was true.

The general manager never tried to include me in a holiday gangbang and I was never involved in a gangrape at the behest of a bunch of gym rats and I'm not sure I actually saw pedo photos in the dresser at Marcel Rupert Chapman's house. Though, I may have. Sometimes I see what I want to see and sometimes I really see it. It's confusing. The important thing is, Daphne had my back on that one.

What I'm saying is, it's not about revenge— I'm just an evil bitch. So . . .

Ladies, I've told you how to do it, and I'm inviting you to join me.

And men, you gaggle of pricks, you best watch out.

Because you could be the next star of *Queen Boss Slay!*

ABOUT THE AUTHOR

Patrick C. Harrison III (PC3) is an author of horror, splatterpunk, and all forms of speculative fiction. His works include Amazon-bestseller *100% Match* and the Splatterpunk Award-nominated novella *Grandpappy*, as well as *The Dark Side of Hell*, *A Savage Breed*, and *Vampire Nuns Behind Bars*. PC3's short stories can be found in numerous anthologies and collections. He resides in Wolfe City, Texas with his family and doggo.

Printed in Great Britain
by Amazon